HOPE

AND

TRUTH

Titles in Between The Lines:

HOPE AND TRUTH
DANIEL BLYTHE

KISS THE SKY
DANIEL BLYTHE

REFUGEE KID
CATHERINE BRUTON

ANNIE
TOMMY DONBAVAND

PROMISE ME
ANN EVANS

SILENT VALLEY
CLIFF McNISH

MADE
KATE ORMAND

SIREN SONG
JACQUELINE RAYNER

Badger Publishing Limited, Oldmedow Road, Hardwick Industrial Estate, King's Lynn PE30 4JJ

Telephone: 01438 791037

www.badgerlearning.co.uk

HOPE AND TRUTH

DANIEL BLYTHE

Badger
LEARNING

Hope and Truth **ISBN** 978-1-78837-209-1

Text © Daniel Blythe 2017
Complete work © Badger Publishing Limited 2017

Publisher: Susan Ross
Senior Editor: Danny Pearson
Editorial Coordinator: Claire Morgan
Copyeditor: Cambridge Publishing Management
Designer: Bigtop Design Ltd
Cover: © Oleg Zabielin / Alamy Stock Photo

4 6 8 10 9 7 5

CHAPTER 1
SAM

Two Days Before

The helicopters were low in the sky. Giant, black, shiny creatures, like a swarm. Chugging and clattering over rooftops and towers, banking and swooping.

Sam Rafford watched them as he made his way down the hill to college, his rucksack over one shoulder.

He wondered what the helicopters could see. How closely they could scan the town, the streets and the houses. Could they pick out individuals, mark them out as troublemakers? Three months ago he'd have thought this was ridiculous. Now it seemed a lot less stupid. It was odd, how quickly people got used to new situations.

As he made his way down the hill, he took his phone out and watched the video Cait had messaged him. It was jerky and poor quality, but there was no mistaking what it showed. The video had been filmed from the middle of a crowd. A caption said O2 ARENA. Many people had one hand raised in the air, as if at a concert. But these people were not holding up lighters or phones. They had their arms stiffly upwards at 45 degrees. You didn't need to know a lot of history to recognise that gesture, Sam thought.

"What on earth are you watching, Sammy?"

He glanced up at his friend Jas's mildly accusing voice. He flicked the video off with his thumb. He didn't know why he felt guilty watching it — there was no reason to — but right now an explanation would have been needed, and he didn't feel like giving one.

"Just people," he said.

"End-Timers."

She had guessed.

He nodded, putting the phone away. "They're making it worse. As if all the stuff on the news wasn't bad enough."

"Mena says they're like fascists."

Sam smiled. "Your girlfriend's a pretty good judge of character."

There was another message after the video. He opened it. It contained just two words: LAST PARTY.

Sam frowned. What did that mean? He would have to ask Cait.

He grinned. Any excuse to talk to her.

At the end of the street leading to school, the barriers were in place. They were a recent addition.

Police officers in hi-vis jackets were checking everyone's ID. The ones doing the checking were not armed, but there were some in the background who were — patrolling up and down in armour, eyes scanning the crowd.

Neither Sam nor Jas nor any of their friends found this odd any more. It was just one of many 'emergency procedures' that the Government had slowly, steadily put into place, telling people it was for their own safety. Cameras in every classroom in school. Random spot-checks in the street. A ban on particular words and phrases on social media and internet forums.

Sam showed his pass — a simple rectangle of white plastic with a barcode. It beeped when held against the police officer's radar, and he was waved through to the school gate.

Jas followed, holding hers up in the same way.

There was a loud warbling sound, which made Sam turn round in alarm.

"Jas? What's up?"

The girl looked frightened, confused. The police officer held up the reader again. "Try it again, love," he said in a kindly, weary voice. "Probably playing up."

Jas held her pass up again, and the same warbling sound echoed through the street. People behind her in the queue were looking at one another uneasily.

"Just step aside there for a minute, would you, love?" said the police officer. "Not sure I can let you through while it's doing that."

"But I've got school!" she snapped.

"Just step aside, please."

Sam had turned back on himself, returned to the barrier, against the tide of blue blazers. "What's up? What's going on?"

"It'll all get sorted," said the police officer with the kindly voice. "We get two or three of these every day. Just means it's picked something up, that's all."

"Picked something up?" said Jas in alarm. "Like what?"

Another police officer had appeared behind her and gently took her arm. "Could you come and step over here, please? We'll go through some questions and get this sorted out."

Sam watched helplessly as Jas was taken away. He knew he ought to speak out, to say something.

But he also knew he was more use on this side of the barrier.

Assembly was at nine o'clock sharp. The headmaster strode on stage, and everyone stood as always, as they knew they had to. He nodded once, which was the signal for everyone to be seated again.

Sam looked around. All the usual faces he had
known since Year 7. Including Cait — down
the end of the row. She had not spotted him yet.
He wanted to thank her for the video of the
End-Timer rally.

Back when they started at this school, things had
been very different. Carefree. No barriers, no
helicopters, no CCTV in the classrooms, none of
the bans and rules that were in place now.

There had been two terrorist incidents in London
in the last two months — major explosions in
Whitehall and Hyde Park. He knew that a third
device at Charing Cross had been found and
defused. His dad had been among those evacuated
from the station.

All of that, combined with the very dangerous
international situation between the USA, China
and North Korea, meant that the city — in fact,
the whole country — was on high alert.

This morning on the breakfast news he had seen
the Prime Minister, her face pale and drawn under

her steely cap of hair, getting on a plane to go to Geneva for talks. 'Last chance' talks, they called it.

The headmaster's voice droned on. Sam was not really paying attention.

"…trust that you will all keep a watch in these difficult times. I would also ask you to report anything you may see that is suspicious, or unusual."

The usual stuff. Alongside the strangely normal information about the football team, the chess club, the arrangement for the mock exams.

Life going on as usual. It ought to be comforting, but it wasn't.

He risked a glance at Cait. She was looking down, but she looked up, briefly, from under her heavy eyelashes. She almost smiled. Then she looked away.

Before the first lesson, Sam broke off from his group and went to the reception desk at the office.

"Yes, love?"

He didn't recognise the secretary on duty. She was older than the usual one, with glasses on a chain.

"I was just wondering if you could tell me about Jasmine Mohindra. If she's coming in today. She got stopped at the barrier."

"Let me have a look," said the woman, and turned to her computer. "What was the name? Spell it for me?"

He did so, waiting impatiently. Everyone was heading up the stairs now to their lessons. In orderly fashion. Teachers with radios stood at the head of the stairs, watching. His unusual behaviour would have been clocked.

The secretary shook her head. "Sorry, love. Nobody of that name goes to this school."

"What?" Sam was shocked. "That can't be right. Jas Mohindra! She's in my form. Dark hair, glasses, about this high." He held his hand about a metre and a half off the ground. "Plays netball."

The secretary spread her hands. "No record. Sorry."

"That's just crazy," said Sam.

"Rafford!"

It was the firm, bellowing voice of Mr Archer, the assistant headteacher. Calling from the top of the stairs.

"Samuel Rafford! Get to your lesson, please! One minute of changeover left!"

His mind reeling in shock, he hurried to the stairs, with a brief, mumbled, "Sorry, sir," as he passed Mr Archer.

Something wasn't right.

And he still hadn't asked Cait what 'Last Party' was all about.

CHAPTER 2

HOPE

Year 0+14, 3 Months and 2 Days

It was a strong Gathering in Sanctuary Base tonight. The most people Hope had seen in some time. They slowly filled the stone pews. Candle-lanterns cast flickering shadows in the huge cavern.

The girls, like Hope and Violet, all had their heads covered, and wore plain, simple dresses that ended just below the knee. The older women were allowed to be bare-headed, although some still chose to wear hats or hoods. The men and boys wore rough, simple, mud-coloured jackets and trousers. Everyone was pale and glossy, their eyes bulging and fish-like.

They looked like people who lived underground.

Because they always had.

This place — Sanctuary — was an underground network of caverns, sealed off from the world above. There were lifts to the surface, but you could only use these if you were a Scavenger, or had an official pass from the Mentors.

Brogan, the Chief Mentor, climbed the rusty stairs to the podium — as usual, to loud applause that echoed through the cavern. He was a tall, thin, bald man with long arms and legs, and wore a pinstriped suit underneath his woollen cloak.

Hope didn't understand why and how Brogan always knew so much. She didn't know how he always had information to give them. But she was glad he did. She gazed into the candle flame as Brogan's words washed over them. She heard Violet draw a sharp breath beside her.

"The dangers on the surface, my friends, remain," said Brogan gravely, his hands folded together in front of him as always. "Our brave teams of Scavengers have been out six times so far this year, and they're going to be going out again, a seventh time. But you must understand that circumstances are… well, very bad."

Hope had very little memory of her real parents. She knew that they had handed her over to the Mentors at the age of four, and waved her off in the trucks taking people to Sanctuary.

"Some of you ask," Brogan went on, his stern eyes watching the crowd, "if we will ever be allowed to return to the surface. Brothers and Sisters, I understand why you ask this. I share your rage, and your pain. I can only give you the same assurance I always give."

He paused for dramatic effect. There was silence in the cold cavern.

"We will return," said Brogan softly, and then he raised his voice — not shouting, just speaking loudly and clearly, obviously in charge. "We *will* return, but only when it is safe to do so!"

There was agreement in the crowd. Nodding of heads. "We, and the other Sanctuaries across the world, have a great responsibility," Brogan said. "We will, at some point, be able to emerge, and remake the world in our image. But not until it is safe to do so."

He pointed at the old-fashioned film projector, and one of the Brothers got up, bowed, and waited for Brogan's signal.

Hope was used to this weekly ritual. She bowed her head.

"Brothers and Sisters," said Brogan, "please be ready. The flames of life."

They all held up their lanterns. The shadows danced and twisted on the wall of the cavern.

"*The flames of life*," chanted the crowd.

"*The darkness of war*," said Brogan.

"*The darkness of war*," repeated the crowd, and together they blew out their flames. Spirals of smoke curled upwards. The smell of hot wax hit Hope's nostrils. As always she focused on the soft glow of the wick, watching it fade to nothing.

"And now let us look once again upon the End Time," said Brogan from the shadows.

As if by magic, a square of flickering light appeared on the stone wall. Hope knew what to expect. There were several of these moving stories — all kept stored in film cans deep in the coolest lower levels of Sanctuary Base. It was never the same one twice in a row, but they always told the same basic story.

The picture jumped and flickered — it had been played many times, and was almost totally bleached of colour.

There were the leaders, shaking their fists. The

tall one climbing the steps to his plane, turning to face the crowd, smiling as if unsure. The woman, looking hunted and alone among her advisors. Speaking to reporters, although they could not hear her words.

Now the great ships, cutting through the ocean. And the coming of the aeroplanes. Opening their bomb bay doors one by one, like great birds of prey ready to swoop.

And then, the images of the Ending. Aeroplanes crashing into towers. Great tidal waves, sweeping though cities. Statues brought crashing down by angry mobs. Crowds chanting in the streets, angrily waving fists. Some holding guns.

The fade to white.

Always, the fade to white.

Then blackness.

There was a moment's peace, the still time. Hope

thought it went on a little longer each time.

"Let your lights shine in the darkness," said Brogan, as he always did.

One by one, the lanterns were re-lit, casting a soft, orange glow across the cavern, bringing robes and faces and hands back to life. Beside Hope, Violet smiled shyly as Hope helped her to re-light hers.

They filed out, through the tunnels, to their various tasks. Some would go to Scavenging duties, others to work on the machinery or the many underground gardens.

Sanctuary extended a long way into the mountain, Hope knew, and she had not seen it all as of yet, even after years down here.

In the tunnel, Violet grabbed her arm. "Look," she said softly.

They hardly ever saw Scavengers in their camouflage suits and gas-masks, so they were a startling sight. They moved almost like ghosts, slow and heavy, strange in the half-light. There were three of them — tall, silvery, each carrying crates.

Their Teacher, Lisbeth, held up her hand at the tunnel junction, stopping them all, and they waited in silence for the Scavengers to pass, to go about their business.

Lisbeth was in her twenties now, so she would have been a teenager when they came down into Sanctuary. She would remember the Old Time.

Hope dreamed of one day becoming a Teacher like Lisbeth, and maybe even growing into a Mentor as the years went on. Maybe — and this was a dream — being the one to lead her people out on to the surface, back into a newer Earth free from disease and radiation.

A new Earth where they could once again live in cities above ground, smell the flowers, hear bees buzzing and eat fruit from trees.

"I need to tell you something," Violet whispered to Hope, almost too quietly to be heard.

"What?" Hope asked, intrigued. "What is it?"

"I can't tell you here," Violet whispered. "You know the Minus Levels?"

Hope nodded. The lowest caverns, used just for storage and power. Hardly anyone ever went down there.

"Meet me in Minus Ten, at the access corridor, tomorrow afternoon after teaching."

"Why? What —"

Hope broke off.

Lisbeth had turned around and was staring at them.

The Teacher lifted a finger to her lips, and the girls, ashamed, bowed their heads and were silent.

But Hope already had the message. She knew what to expect and what to do.

And she needed to know more.

CHAPTER 3
SAM
One Day Before

The TV news showed helicopter footage of aircraft carriers slicing through the blue sea, the waves behind them crisp and clear.

Sam, leaning forwards on the sofa, counted 10, 11, 12 ships.

"I don't know why you watch this," said Cait, popping a chocolate into her mouth as she sat beside him. "It's just depressing."

Sam glanced at her. He was well aware of the irony. Here he was, at home. Mum and Dad out, and just him and Cait Morland on the sofa.

She had come round with a clear excuse —
something about borrowing a book — and
yet instead he was watching the 24-hour
news channel.

"It's really important," he said. "And it affects my
dad's job."

"Yeah… what does he do exactly?" asked Cait.

"Government liaison."

"What does that mean?"

"Well, I can't really say." He turned the volume
up. "I want to hear this."

The newsreader's voice was crisp, clear and calm.

"*As the United States taskforce moves closer to North
Korean waters, the Chinese government today repeated that
they would consider any shots fired to be an act of war.
The President, meanwhile, is understood to be leaving his
summer residence for the White House…*"

The President of the United States appeared on screen, waving to crowds from the top of the steps leading to Air Force One.

His face did not wear its usual smug expression. He looked grim and hard-set, and his hair appeared to have turned snow-white overnight.

"Ugh," said Cait, shuddering. "He's so *awful*. A snake. Turn him off."

"Do you get what's going on?" Sam asked.

She slid a little closer to him, twirling her hair. "I dunno. My mum and dad talked about this. Living with the threat of war all the time…. Never thought it would happen to us." She seemed to be weighing something up, thinking about something.

"What is it?" he asked. He was painfully aware of how close she was now.

She leaned over so that her mouth was against his ear.

"Last Party," she whispered.

"The video," said Sam. "What… what's it about?"

"I can't say here," Cait murmured.

"Really?" Sam was interested straight away.

"Check your inbox," she said, and now she looked nervous. She was reaching for her jacket. "Look, I've got to go. I promised my dad I'd be back."

"Can't you text him?"

She shook her head. "Not with the way things are."

"OK…. See you later, then?" Sam said, trying not to sound too disappointed.

"OK."

"Cait," he said as she was turning to leave.

"Yes, Sam?" Her eyes were wide, questioning.

"Cait, do you know what happened to Jas?"

Cait frowned. "Jas? Jas who?"

"Jasmine Mohindra. From our year in school. She's just disappeared. And so has her girlfriend, Mena — I checked."

Cait shook her head. "No idea. But I wouldn't dwell on it, Sam. You know the drill. If she's disappeared, she was probably trouble."

He didn't like the casual, accepting way Cait said that. It was chilling. There was a time — not so long ago — when a disappearance would have been massive news. Not anymore.

After Cait had gone, he flicked through the TV channels. He had noticed that there were fewer of them these days.

The children's cartoons, the shopping channels — they had all gone, as had a lot of the free internet stuff.

There were more channels full of old stuff these days, called things like 'Olden Days' and 'Vintage', showing reassuring dramas and documentaries from years gone by. There was even 'Best of British', which seemed to be all about how wonderful life had been in black and white. Sam had snorted in disgust when he first saw this.

Outside, helicopters clattered in the sky. Sam went to the window. Dozens of them. More than he had ever seen before.

His phone buzzed. He looked at it.

The message read:

LAST PARTY.

And then there was another message. This one gave a time, and a place, to be picked up.

CHAPTER 4

HOPE

Year 0+14, 3 Months and 3 Days

They met in a cavern that was lit by the softest natural glow. Deep in the rocks, it cast a green hue over everything.

Hope was there first. She waited patiently for Violet. She counted the seconds. She remembered her mother having a little clock on her wrist at one point. That was one of the flashes of the Old Time that came back to her now and then.

She was sure she could also remember being in a playpen, having coloured fluffy animals spinning above her on a mobile. She had mentioned this to Lisbeth once. Lisbeth had pulled a face, and told her it was best not to remember any of that.

And then she said that it might be a false memory anyway. Hope was not sure what that meant.

Violet's shadow appeared first, then the girl herself, carrying a lantern. She glanced over her shoulder, worriedly.

"He said he'd be here."

"Who?" asked Hope. "You haven't told me what this is all about, Violet."

The younger girl lowered her eyes, perhaps shy or worried. "I've been hearing these things for weeks now," she said. "But Frederick…. He said he had proof. Absolute proof."

"Proof of what?" hissed Hope. She was aware that her voice sounded horribly loud in the rocky passage.

"Hello?"

It was a young man's voice.

Violet grabbed Hope's arm. There were footsteps above them, on the metal stairs leading down to the cavern. They watched as the new arrival came into view.

He was a tall boy, blond and sharp-faced, about Hope's age. Hope recognised his face, but did not know his name — there were 800 people in Sanctuary, and she had by no means spoken to them all.

"Frederick," said Violet in relief. "You made it."

"We don't have long," said the boy. "I need to show you this. Violet — put the lantern down on that rock."

There was a flat rock nearby, like a low table. Violet put the lantern on it. Frederick glanced over his shoulder.

"They can't know I'm gone," he said. "I've got about five minutes."

"Where do you work?" Hope asked.

"In the Guardian Corps. I found this yesterday."
He took a small, folded piece of newspaper out of
his pocket and spread it out on the flat rock. The
girls peered at it curiously. "Can you both read?"
Frederick asked.

"Of course," Hope snapped. "We're not stupid."

It was, at first glance, an ordinary story. It was
about a middle-aged woman called Susan
winning something called the 'National Lottery'
and donating it all to the poor. There was a
photograph of her with a glass of some fizzy
drink, smiling at the camera and holding an
enormous piece of card saying NATIONAL
BANK OF LONDON, and a number.

Hope blinked, counting all the zeroes. It was a
very big number. She thought the woman had
kind eyes.

"So it's an old newspaper," said Hope, shrugging.
"What's important about that?"

"Look at the date," said Frederick.

They did.

And Hope's world turned upside down.

CHAPTER 5

SAM

The Day

The old sea-fort was heaving with young people, dancing, laughing, kissing. Sam Rafford had never seen anything like it.

"What is this?" he said to Cait, as they were pushed forwards. "It's like an End-Timer riot!"

The heat hit Sam as soon as they entered the echoing space. He was still getting over coming here by helicopter and boat. Cait's dad knew some high-up people, but he had not realised the scale of this thing.

It was a party to end all parties.

A party for the end of the world.

About, he guessed, 300 young people had
gathered in the vast central space of the sea-fort.
It was like a giant, steel box, with large screens
around displaying music videos and swirling
patterns of light. It was so hot that even the walls
were sweaty.

There was a DJ on a podium, his face shaded by
a silver cap. The place shook to old-school tunes:
house and hip-hop, even some vintage disco.
It was as if he was trying to play something for
everyone, as if he knew it might be the last time
he played anything at all. Sam could feel the
bass thumping in every surface, rattling his teeth.
People were openly embracing, lifting bottles high
in the air. Some people were crying.

They were cheering, stomping now.

Sam saw that the images on the screen had
changed. They were no longer music videos or
swirling patterns. They were pictures from the

news. Ships cutting their way through grey oceans. Helicopters landing, soldiers marching.

It looked like war.

There was no soundtrack, but the party made the sound, a great, angry roar of life and love.

Sam was both excited and terrified.

He leaned over to Cait, who had already found two friends and was laughing along with them.

"It's like it really is the end!" he shouted into her ear. "Like you really knew!"

She leaned round to him. "Of course!" she yelled in his ear. She slipped her arms around his neck. "Come here."

The cheering and stomping abruptly stopped.

There was a deathly silence. Then there were shouts, jeers, catcalls. The crowd in the hall steamed and shook with anger.

Sam looked round in alarm, almost forgetting that Cait had been about to kiss him. "What's happening?" he asked. "Is this it?"

"The President," he heard someone say.

The face of the President of the United States looked large on the biggest screen, high above the DJ. The steel box echoed to boos and hisses, growing louder and louder. But someone cranked up the volume, so his voice bellowed out through the enormous speakers. Like the voice of a god, or a demon.

"*I stand before you,*" the President was saying, "*safe in the knowledge that we have done everything we can. We must not rest. You folks know I'm telling you the truth.*"

You folks, thought Sam angrily. He spoke to the whole world like he was talking to a barn dance.

The camera swung round now to a sterner, more serious face. Sam recognised the Secretary-General of the United Nations.

He was reading a prepared statement.

The Last Party was still watching, almost silent, and waiting as the words washed over them like a tidal wave.

And in the distance, Sam could hear the sound of approaching helicopters.

CHAPTER 6
HOPE
Year 0+14, 3 Months and 4 Days

"I don't like this," Hope said to Violet.

Violet did not respond. They glided through the torchlit passageways, trying to look as if deep in meditation, or at least deep in thought. They kept their heads down, and their hands folded together.

They passed the occasional Teacher in their long red robes, and at one point a bearded Mentor in his dark suit. The Mentor frowned at them, but allowed them to pass.

After what seemed like an eternity walking through the passageways, they arrived at a dark tunnel leading to one of the underground rivers.

Hope could feel the cool rush of the water on her face. She could see there was a rope bridge across the river, leading to a rusty metal ladder.

"This is the place," Violet whispered.

"I'd expected it to be guarded," Hope said. "I don't like this."

They cast fearful looks around. Hope hitched up her long robe, held her lantern high and followed Violet across the creaking rope bridge.

*

She'd had a bad feeling about this from the start.

Why had Frederick chosen to share the information with them? Violet, though, had assured her that it was fine. She knew Frederick. He was one of the Old Families, very trustworthy. She had spoken with him before, and he had shown kindness to her at difficult times.

Hope had to trust that Violet was a good judge of character.

The Teachers had spent years telling them of the wars that had wrecked and poisoned their world. Stories about bad men flying aircraft into glass towers, of bombs dropping on children. Of whole towns destroyed.

The story of how the people of Sanctuary had finally come together and, two days before the terror led the world into chaos, they had sealed themselves inside these cave systems, not knowing how, or even if, they would come out.

They learned of how the Mentors, who had been people in high-up places in the world above, had planned for this day. They had used their funds to create the world's four Sanctuary Bases for survival. Money for renewable power. Money for stocks of food.

The Sanctuary Bases had been ready when needed. When the day came. And the day had been a day of war, a day of peace talks going badly wrong and of armies advancing on capital cities.

Hope had only been a small child when they had gone underground. She barely remembered the greenery, the natural light. The blue sky. She had seen them many times since on videos. Four days after they had gone into Sanctuary — she knew this because she had been told — the End Time had come.

But if what Frederick had shown the girls yesterday was true, then the world above was not a barren place at all. It was not a world of radiation, of destroyed cities.

It was a world where people carried on their normal lives in towns and cities — living, breathing, loving, eating, drinking. Where the papers could talk about something as trivial — as everyday — as a woman drinking a glass of something fizzy because she had won a lottery and was giving the money away.

The End Time could be a lie.

Which meant one thing.

They were being kept down here for a different reason.

"He's not coming," Hope said. "Let's go back. It could be a trap."

Violet held up a hand. "No. Listen!"

Footsteps. A tall, spiky shadow on the wall. And there he was — Frederick. As promised.

"I'm sorry I'm late," he said, and nodded first to Violet, then to Hope. "It was hard to get away." He glanced behind him once. "I bribed the Guardians who normally patrol here."

"So… where are we going?" Hope asked.

Frederick smiled, and lifted one long, bony finger. He pointed upwards.

"They've been lying all this time, Hope. There was no End Time. After the towers fell, there were wars, and terrorism, and terrible things happened, but… the world carried on."

"I want to believe you," she said, her head spinning. She felt as if she was in a dream.

"You want to find the truth?" Frederick said. "The truth is up there."

"What is this?" Hope asked, looking at the rusty metal ladder. She leaned inside the shaft and looked up. "Does this really lead to the surface?"

"Not directly. But follow me."

And he smiled.

Frederick went up the ladder first, followed by Hope, with Violet bringing up the rear. They tied their lanterns to their belts so that they could be safe but could still see.

Up and up they climbed. The rungs seemed endless to Hope. Her hands were sweaty, slippery on the metal. She could see no sign of any light from above.

It seemed to Hope that they had been climbing for hours when finally she heard Frederick shouting from above, "OK, over the top now! Come on!"

She saw his lantern light disappear then reappear at another angle. He was leaning. He was looking at them over the lip of the shaft.

He helped Hope up, his hand firm and strong on her arm. Violet followed. As Frederick helped Violet straighten up, Hope swung her lantern around the chamber they were in, and gasped.

It seemed to have been hollowed out of the bare earth. It smelt damper and warmer than the caverns of Sanctuary.

And set into the earth above her, at an angle of 45 degrees, was a metal hatch, about five square metres.

"Is this it?" she said, amazed.

"If you want," said Frederick. The tone of his voice seemed to have changed. "See, Mr Brogan?" he called over his shoulder. "I never let you down. I've brought you the agents of your destruction."

Hope's gasped out loud as the dark-suited Brogan emerged from the shadows, armed and helmeted Guardians behind him.

Violet shrank back into Hope, shaking in fear.

Hope stared at Frederick in anger. The boy's face was hard and cold. Just like any other Guardian, now. His arms were folded. He gave her a cold, unfriendly smile.

"Traitors to Sanctuary, Mr Brogan," said Frederick. "Yours to do with as you wish."

Brogan nodded. He pointed to the guards, and they stepped forwards. They raised their rifles at Hope and Violet.

Hope stepped forwards. "Let Violet go. *Please*. She's too young."

Brogan's expression didn't change.

There was a loud, metallic bang in the chamber.

Hope closed her eyes, expecting pain and death.

Nothing.

Hardly daring, she opened her eyes.

Frederick, Brogan, Violet and the Guardians were looking up at the hatch, where the sound had come from.

It happened again. BANG.

And again, three times. Three loud bangs, one after another.

Smoke began to drift from the edges where the hatch met the earth. A metal crowbar appeared, forcing the lowest edge of the hatch upwards.

Brogan stepped forwards, his face twisted in fury. "No. Noooo! What is this?"

Frederick stepped forwards, putting himself between Brogan and the girls. "I thought it was time" he said, "to get a message to the outside world. The *real* outside world." He glanced at Hope, and smiled. "Time for all this to be over."

And then there was a great creaking and grinding of metal, as the hatchway opened.

Hope shielded her eyes from a bright, hot burst of sunlight. Figures were framed against the light, men with guns. She could smell the fresh earth, and heard the angry barking of dogs.

She knew, now, that nothing would ever be the same again.

CHAPTER 7
SAM
The Day After

"*...this fragile, but still stable hope for peace,*" the Prime Minister was saying on the TV.

She paused, looked around. Her mouth was grim and set, but the stress of the last few weeks seemed to have lifted from her. She seemed more in control. There were still armed police behind her at the door of Downing Street, but only two rather than the whole squad there had been before.

Sam held his breath. He looked round at his mother and father. They were smiling for the first time in many weeks. They were hanging on the Prime Minister's every word.

He didn't understand entirely what had happened. But he knew one thing. The world had come to the brink, and had pulled back. Politics had won over war. Just.

He had heard the Secretary-General's statement, on the giant speakers of the Last Party. It had not been a grim statement of war, as they had expected. It had been a brief but cautious speech about successful talks. The language of people coming together. Of people working towards peace.

The world was, for the moment, not going to end.

Not today.

He flicked to another channel. It, too, was news — but it was showing a different story.

"The so-called Sanctuary cult, it is only now emerging, is believed to have kept several hundred people living a lie for over ten years," said the reporter.

The footage being shown was juddery, poor-quality. Sam imagined it had been shot from a helicopter, as it appeared to be offering a view from about twenty metres up in the air.

The shot showed a large, steel hatchway set into the side of a hill. Beside it, there was a pile of torn grass and burnt black earth. It looked as if the hatchway had been hidden, and was now revealed.

"The members of the so-called Sanctuary cult began to emerge just after six o'clock yesterday morning."

There were armed men in black surrounding the hatchway. Some of them were going in, now, helping people out. Some would not come out, and had to be persuaded.

Sam watched in fascination. The people were wrapped in long, army-style camouflage coats and hoods. They all wore gas masks, as if they were scared of being poisoned by the air. As they emerged, they appeared dazzled by the natural light, and the soldiers gave them tinted glasses to wear under their masks.

One of the girls looked straight into the camera. Straight at Sam, or so it seemed. Her hand went to her mouth.

Sam seemed to feel what she was feeling. To know what she was discovering, there, in that moment.

That the world had a future.

That darkness could sometimes lead to light.

He smiled at the girl on the screen, lifted his mug of tea. "OK, then," he said. "Let's see what happens."

THE END

ABOUT THE AUTHOR

Daniel Blythe is the author of 22 books, including several of the Doctor Who novels, as well as *Shadow Runners* and *Emerald Greene and the Witch Stones*. He is originally from Maidstone, but now lives with his wife and teenage children in Yorkshire. He has been published in 12 countries including the USA, Germany and Brazil, and he has led writing days and workshops in over 400 schools.